W9-BDH-495

To Christy Ottaviano, Louise May, Melanie Donovan,
David Gershator, and David M. Gershater
—P. G.

To my first brand-new granddaughter, Pia,
and her parents, Giselle and Kieran
—M. P.

Author's Note

These slumber-song images are collected from Africa,
Spain, and the Caribbean. I'm indebted to Dr. Afam E. Ebeogu for
her work in collecting and explicating Nigerian nursery songs and lullabies.

Henry Holt and Company, LLC, *Publishers since 1866*
115 West 18th Street, New York, New York 10011
www.henryholt.com

Henry Holt is a registered trademark of Henry Holt and Company, LLC

Text copyright © 2004 by Phillis Gershator. Illustrations copyright © 2004 by Mélisande Potter.
All rights reserved. Distributed in Canada by H. B. Fenn and Company Ltd.

Library of Congress Cataloging-in-Publication Data
Gershator, Phillis. The babysitter sings / by Phillis Gershator; illustrated by Mélisande Potter.
Summary: A babysitter sings a rhyming song to reassure the child.
[1. Babysitters—Fiction. 2. Bedtime—Fiction. 3. Separation anxiety—Fiction.
4. Lullabies—Fiction. 5. Stories in rhyme.] I. Potter, Mélisande, ill. II. Title.
PZ8.3.G3235Bab 2004   [E]—dc21   2003002532

Designed by Martha Rago / ISBN 0-8050-7199-7 / First Edition—2004
Printed in the United States of America on acid-free paper. ∞
1 3 5 7 9 10 8 6 4 2
The artist used ink and gouache on Strathmore
watercolor paper to create the illustrations for this book.

The Babysitter Sings

by

Phillis Gershator

illustrated by

Mélisande Potter

Henry Holt and Company

New York

NORTHPORT PUBLIC LIBRARY
NORTHPORT, NEW YORK

Baby cheeps like a bird,
and I know why.
When Mama and Papa go out,
Baby starts to cry.

Hush, little bird.
I'll sing you a song.
Do you want to know
where Papa's gone?

Papa's gone fishing
for fish in the sea
to bring home a fish
for Baby and me.

Hush, *little bird.*
I'll sing you a song.
Do you want to know
where Mama's gone?

Mama's gone to market,
to market to buy
bean cakes for Baby,
so Baby won't cry.

Hush, *little bird*.
Do you want to play?
See all the birdies fly away!

Little bird, don't fly away.
Here's the monkey's bangle.
Here's the monkey's little bell.
Jingle, jingle, jangle.

If you fly, I'll follow you
all around the town.
Take a step—one, two, three.

All

fall

down!

Little bird, say hello to me.
Nod your head hello.

Little bird, say good-bye to me.
Where will you go?

Ba Ba

Hush, *little bird.*
Now what's wrong?
Is the little bird
crying for another song?

Birdie cries when it's dark.
Birdie cries when it's light.
Birdie wants me to sing
all day and all night!

*I sing about the jungle
where the lion sleeps
near a tall tree where
a little bird cheeps.*

*I sing about the cow
who moos all day
and the dove who
spreads her wings*
and flies away.

Hush, little bird.
Fold up your wings.
Close your eyes
when the babysitter sings.

Mama's coming home.
Papa won't be long.
Hush, little bird.
I'll sing you one more song.

Oh, where is sleep?
Is it hiding in the trees,
perched like a bird
in the dark, dark leaves?

Where is sleep?
Does it crawl? Does it creep?
Is it coming closer?
Don't make a peep.

Good Night

Sleep will find you.
Yes, it will.

JUL 2004

Northport - E. Northport Public Library
151 Laurel Avenue
Northport, N. Y. 11768
261-6930